SCOOBY-DOO!

on

Werewolf Watch

Written by Sonia Sander
Illustrated by Duendes del Sur

SCHOLASTIC INC.
New York Toronto London Auckland
Sydney Mexico City New Delhi Hong Kong

ISBN 978-0-545-38477-3

SCOOBY-DOO and all related characters and elements are trademarks of and © Hanna-Barbera.

Published by Scholastic Inc. All rights reserved.

SCHOLASTIC and associated logos are trademarks and/or registered trademarks of Scholastic Inc.

Lexile® is a registered trademark of MetaMetrics, Inc.

12 11 10 9 8 7 6 5 4 3 2   12 13 14 15 16/0

Designed by Michael Massen

Printed in the U.S.A.   40

First printing, January 2012

Scooby and the gang were visiting Pippa's Pet Shop.

The shop door opened. *Ding-a-ling!*

"Welcome!" Pippa said. "I'm so glad you're going to help us this week."

Pippa showed the gang around.

"This is Max," said Pippa. "He helps me in the shop."

"Jinkies," said Velma. "It looks like you have your hands full. How did you get so much fur on you?"

"Some days are just messier than others," said Max.

"Working in a pet shop is a piece of cake," said Shaggy.

"Aren't these baby animals just the cutest things?" asked Daphne.

"Ruh?!" asked Scooby.

"Don't worry, Scooby," said Velma. "None of them are as cute as you."

"Like, I'm great at this grooming thing," said Shaggy.

Scooby and the puppies didn't agree.

"*Ree-hee-hee*," chuckled Scooby. Baby chicks were tickling him!

"Like, the chicks think you're their mother, Scoob," said Shaggy.

Shaggy was laughing so hard, he fell into the dog wash!

Fred, Daphne, and Velma giggled when
they saw Shaggy's doggie hairdo.

The next day, there was a big surprise waiting for Scooby and the gang.

Every animal in the pet shop was running loose!

"Jeepers! How on earth did all the animals escape?" asked Daphne.

"I don't know," said Pippa. "Nothing like this has ever happened before."

"There's no time to waste, gang," called Fred. "Start picking up the animals!"

Scooby and Shaggy rounded up the snakes, lizards, spiders, and crabs.

"Like, look out!" cried Shaggy. "The faster we lock up these creepy crawlers, the better!"

"Ruh-huh!" agreed Scooby.

"Thank you for helping me clean up this mess," said Pippa. "I just don't get who or what is doing this to my shop."

"Looks like we've got a mystery to solve," said Fred. "Let's spend the night in the pet shop."

"Jeepers, Max," said Daphne. "The sole of your shoe is red, too."

"Oh, um, I must have stepped in it," said Max, hiding his shoe.

Scooby and Shaggy were not too happy
about spending the night.
So Velma said they could do puppy patrol.

"*Row-ow-ow!*" Scooby howled at the moon along with the puppies.

Only there weren't just puppies in the pen.

"Zoinks! A werewolf!" said Shaggy. "Run, Scooby! Run!"

It wasn't long before the werewolf was chasing the whole gang.

"Like, I was afraid something like this would happen," cried Shaggy. "That wicked weirdo is getting closer. Now what do we do?"

"Quick, this way!" called Fred. "We can hide in the storeroom."

Inside the storeroom, the gang found a few clues.
"Jinkies, this red paint is the same color as the writing on the wall," said Velma.
"Why would a pet shop have fake fur?" asked Daphne.
"It's about time we set a trap for this werewolf," said Fred. "This dog washing machine is giving me an idea. . . ."

"Jeepers, this soap is slippery," said Daphne. "With any luck, the werewolf will find it slippery, too," said Fred. "It'll make him slide right into our trap."

"Like, why do I get the feeling Scooby and I are going to be the bait?" whined Shaggy.

Fred's plan worked.
"*O-O-O-O-W-W-W!*" howled the werewolf
as he slid across the soapy floor.
He flew right into the soapy water.
SPLASH!

"Okay, gang," called Fred. "Grab a brush, and let's get cleaning. It's time to find out who's behind this mystery."

"I think I already know who the werewolf is," said Velma. "We've seen this fake fur and footprints from this red sneaker before."

Velma was right! The werewolf was Max!
"How could you do this to me, Max?"
asked Pippa.

"I didn't mean to hurt anyone. I was just having a little fun," said Max.

"I wanted you to pay me more. I thought you'd give me a raise when you saw how much you needed me."

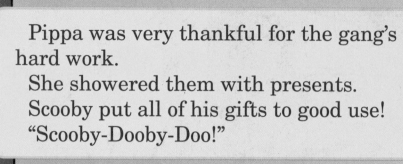

Pippa was very thankful for the gang's
hard work.
She showered them with presents.
Scooby put all of his gifts to good use!
"Scooby-Dooby-Doo!"